A Vacant Room

JANE COMER

ISBN-13: 978-0-9885280-0-0

Theatredust Books
Portland, Oregon, USA

"Hear my soul speak:
The very instant that I saw
you, did
My heart fly to your service."

William Shakespeare

Three Tales of Connection

A Vacant Room

April, 1979

The class bell rang out, and with that the school day was over. Usually this was a good thing. For Claire Adkins, not so much. As she rose from her desk in her last period study hall, it was with complete dread. Gathering her books and her brave smile, she dragged herself out into the halls of her high school.

"It's Claire Adkins, big-time star!" Gary Banister shouted.

Right, Claire thought. Big-time star. If they only knew.

"Can I have your autograph?" Alice Hanover shouted, in absolute mockery.

"You should be so lucky!" Claire shouted back. Mercifully, the distance from her last class to the school parking lot was short. Quickly jamming the key into the door of her red convertible, she climbed behind the wheel. "Please start," she said to the car, knowing there was no guarantee that it would. However, it did start, and she breathed a relieved sigh. Pulling out of the parking lot and onto the street, she had another wish. "Please, car, don't die on me." Fortunately, the convertible did not stall the entire three miles to the radio station where Claire worked.

Everything about her life seemed so impressive to everyone at school. The convertible. The fact that her after school job was being a disc jockey at her town's small radio station. If they only knew, she thought. She still remembered the day she got the job. She had worked up the nerve to see if they had an internship she could do at the station. Claire was a standout of the school speech and debate team, and thought spending an hour or two a week volunteering at the station would look good on her college applications. She was stunned when Randy Magic, the station manager, quickly showed her how to push the right buttons and put her right on the air. Such things are not supposed to happen. But it did, and fast! Randy explained that the person doing the 4:00 PM to 6:00 PM shift had just quit, leaving him in the lurch. And when she showed up to see about the internship, the job was hers.

At first, it was scary and exciting. Making sure she was running the equipment correctly. Picking out country music songs to play. Fighting her nerves when making announcements between the songs. Picking out news stories from the local paper and making a newscast out of them.

Then reality set in. The station was not exactly a ratings leader. Claire wasn't sure how many people listened to the station regularly. She knew of only one. A strange girl named Mouse, who called each time Claire was on the air, usually to ask her to play the same song, "Vacant Room," by a group called the One Hitters. It was a perfect name for this group, for it was their only hit. The station never had any new songs to play; she had been shuffling the same thirty-six recordings repeatedly, including "Vacant Room." And though Claire had worked at the station for three months now, she had only been paid half the money she had earned. Paychecks were distributed by Randy Magic's wife Ricki, and the only thing she did less often than handing out money was bathe. The woman was absolutely rank. Claire never had to turn and look to know Ricki had entered the room.

Other than when Ricki and her aroma entered the room, which was only rarely, Claire felt as if she was broadcasting to no one. It all was pointless. It was like making a speech to a vacant room. And a vacant room was what it usually was. She was playing to vacant room, usually while playing the song "Vacant Room." The station had no technicians or engineers. Claire also had to operate all the equipment, and was usually alone at the station after Steve Gee, the mid day guy left.

"Good afternoon, everybody," Claire said, softly speaking into the microphone. "Welcome to another afternoon of Claire plays the thirty-six hits that were big last year." No longer able to hide her disgust at the radio station, she had taken openly to insulting the place over the air. After all, it wasn't as if anyone was actually listening. The phone rang. It was no surprise, the only time during a shift when any of her phone lines would light up.

"KOLD-FM," Claire answered.

"Hi, Claire, this is Mouse."

"Hi, Mouse."

"You're so funny when you make fun of your radio station. I love it. Can you play 'Vacant Room'?"

"Of course I will, right after the news." Claire glanced at the small pink teddy bear which still sat on a shelf, two weeks after Mouse had won it by calling in to the station. "When are you coming by to pick up your bear? I'm looking forward to finally meeting you face to face."

"My mom's pretty busy. Maybe she'll drive me by to get it tomorrow."

"Well, make sure she does, I'll be happy to see you!"

Thanks, Claire; I'm your biggest fan!"

"Did you get my picture?" Mouse had asked for Claire's picture, and lacking a proper head-shot, she had mailed her one of her senior photos.

"Yes, I did. It's exceptional!"

Mouse hung up, and that was it for human contact for the rest of her shift.

"I just don't know if I can do this radio thing anymore," Claire stated to the boy standing in front of her. It was mid morning break between classes.

Josh, Claire's boyfriend of two years, glanced at her as if she had just thrown food at him. "Claire, I don't see what the problem is," he said. "No matter if they don't pay you, no matter if no one listens, you're still working at a radio station. It doesn't get any cooler than that."

"No one is listening! What's the point?

"I listen!"

"Did you hear the joke I made about the giraffe today?"

"Yeah. Very, very funny."

"Josh, I didn't make a joke about a giraffe today."

"It..., it must have been the other day you said it, then."

"I've never made a giraffe joke in my life. Have you ever listened to my show, or are you lying about that too?"

"Well..."

"That does it; I'm quitting this stupid radio job."

"Are you serious?"

"Have you even been listening? Yes."

"Well, then, there's something I've been wanting to tell you."

"Josh...."

"I've been thinking we shouldn't be as close as we've been."

"Are you breaking up with me? Please tell me you're not breaking up with me!"

"It's really for the best, Claire," Josh said, as the bell for class rang. "Well, got to go, can't miss class...." Josh took off running.

"Josh, come back here....we need to talk about...." Josh disappeared, as if he did not hear her. Missing class had never been a concern for him before.

The next days dragged by. Josh was not at all shy about suddenly being seen with April Dennis, a sophomore girl. Claire guessed they had been secretly seeing each other for some time. Quitting her radio job would be a good thing. She would have a much better idea how people really felt about her. The question, though, was how to quit. It was proving difficult to find someone to quit to. Randy Magic was on some sort of trip with his brass band, and doing his show by remote. Claire didn't think it right to quit by long distance. And Ricki must have been with him, since she hadn't smelled up the office lately. And her shifts were growing intolerable. Even Mouse had not called in for several days. Eventually Claire decided her only choice would be to simply leave and not come back. After signing off and listening for Randy Magic to take over from his long distance control system, Claire gathered what few things she kept at the station. She then prepared to lock the station doors for the last time. She noticed the prize Mouse had won was still near the door, waiting to be picked up, with the address Clare had taped to it still in place. Figuring her last duty should just as well be delivering the prize the station was too cheap to mail; Claire grabbed the pink teddy bear and carried it to the convertible with her armful of belongings.

She had a difficult enough time driving the unreliable convertible along her regular routes, heading in a strange direction made Claire especially nervous. However, the convertible ran smoother than it had in ages, as if it realized it was on a special mission and could not fail now. Driving through block after block of identical houses in a bland housing development on the outskirts of town, Claire finally pulled into the closed off street that contained the address of Mouse's house, and discovered that someone was having a party. Cars were parked everywhere, far more than one would expect would belong to the handful of houses in that area. However, none of the houses were brightly lit, and the standard loud noises of people shouting echoed nowhere. Finding the house identified by the address, Claire stepped onto the porch, knocking on the door.

"Come in, dear," said the gray-haired older lady who opened the door. The lady owned a face drenched in sorrow, but just a hint of a smile seemed to appear on her face as she looked at Claire.

"Uh, I'm here to see Mouse," Claire said, nervously looking around at the crowd of people in the tiny living room, all whom appeared very sad. Oddly, the mood in the room grew brighter as they saw Claire.

"Please wait here just one moment, Ms. Adkins," the elderly lady said, before disappearing through a door off to the side of the living room.

Before Claire could even try to begin figuring how they seemed to know who she was, a younger woman came through the door. "Quick," she said, without pausing to introduce herself, "she just regained consciousness."

Quickly following the woman, Claire found herself in a quiet little room. The quiet that is only heard in a room where someone is dying. The senior photo Claire had mailed to Mouse was thumb tacked to the wall, explaining how everyone knew who Claire was. And in the small bed, a tiny, bald headed girl lay under the covers. The girl was looking wide eyed at Claire, a large smile on her face. Claire sadly knew the girl was Mouse. “Claire!” the girl exclaimed in a weak voice. “What are you doing here?”

Claire put on her best entertainer attitude, though it was difficult. “Just bringing my number-one fan the prize she won,” Claire said, handing the small pink teddy bear to her.

Mouse delicately took the bear, holding it happily in her arms. “I’m your biggest fan, Claire,” she softly whispered, no longer having the energy to shout it as she used to into the phone. She dropped off asleep, a happy smile still on her face.

“Thank you so much for showing up today, Ms. Adkins,” said the woman who had led her into the room. “It meant the world to my daughter. As you can see, she doesn't have much time left."

And as Claire blinked back her tears, she did see. Soon this bedroom would be a vacant room, making the other vacant rooms in her seem silly.

The next day, the convertible sputtered to a stop in front of the radio station. At least she made it to her destination. She would have to see about finding a way home. But for now, she had another radio show to do.

And Ivy Smiled

ONE

It may have been the middle of September, but Jerry Sebastian's mind was stuck on Mae. Mae Ann Reynolds, that is. She was the dreamiest girl in the junior class at Adams High School, and Jerry was interested in being her guy. Every other guy was desperate to go out with her, but Jerry was only interested. He was never desperate about anything. Being the star off-guard on the varsity basketball team and one of the most popular people in your school means never being desperate about anything. But when it came to Mae, he was interested. He watched as she walked down the high school hallway, her walk so graceful that it seemed her feet never touched the ground. Instead she floated. She was like a living daydream.

"Hey, Jere," Sam Figouri asked, interrupting Jerry's brain lock on Mae, "want to go shoot baskets?"

It was three-twenty PM, classes were over for the day, and normally Jerry would be running for the nearest basketball hoop. But today was different. "Sorry Sam," he glumly answered, "I've got to go straight home today. Mother's orders. We've got company coming." Jerry slammed shut the door to his locker, it was clear he wasn't happy about having to go home early.

"Chill out, Jere. Maybe they'll bring some nice stuff for you. Maybe a new basketball or something."

Jerry looked at Sam disdainfully. All Sam ever thought of was what people could give him, as if getting things was what life was all about. He didn't like Sam very much. "I don't expect them to bring me anything, Sam. It's an old friend of Mother who's broke and needs a place to stay for a while."

"If anybody's got the room, you guys do," Sam said, with a gleam in his eyes.

Jerry's heart felt nothing but contempt for that gleam. Sure, Father was a rich corporate owner-executive, and they lived in a big house. But his life was far from great, and Jerry was tired of the gleams of envy he was always seeing in everybody's eyes. If only everybody could realize how horrible it was being Jerry Sebastian. "I have to run, buddy. Mother said she'd have a fit if I wasn't home as soon as possible," he said, wearing a relaxed, friendly grin. Jerry briskly jogged down the hall and out the door which opened onto the student parking lot. Jumping behind the wheel of his customized 1968 red Mustang, he ripped out of the parking lot, leaving behind burned rubber, and drove off to his parents' home in the SW Portland hills.

Jerry and his family lived in one of the biggest houses in one of the richest neighborhoods in Portland. The beauty of the mansion which he drove toward registered little effect on him, however. It was just the place where he ate, slept, and kept his things. Jerry's family was rich, having founded a wool coat manufacturing company in Portland's pioneer days. Jerry, however, tried not to think about being rich. To him, having money meant never having to worry about it. If only the people at school would stop reminding him that he had it. Pulling into the driveway of the Sebastian estate, Jerry saw his grandmother's Cadillac parked next to his mother's Porsche. He groaned, for if there was anything he hated more than his grandmother, it was having her come for a visit. She was the biggest crab he'd never eaten. "Jeremy, how's my boy?" Grandmother asked as Jerry walked into the front parlor.

Jerry felt like telling the hag to go lick a light socket, but instead replied, "Fine, Grandmother."

Grandmother smiled at Jerry as if he were a reject from a laxative company before returning to the conversation she had been having with Jerry's mother. "Really, Penelope," she said, "I don't know why you have to open your doors to a welfare mother and her lunatic daughter."

"Because, Mother, Ginnie Barnes was my best friend in college and I'm not about to have her and Ivy sleeping on the street." As his mother spoke, Jerry could tell by the red blush in her cheeks that she was just barely controlling her anger. "And Ivy isn't a lunatic. She just has serious emotional troubles."

"That child hasn't spoken a word since she was six. Nine years ago," Grandmother explained. "She's totally unaware of what's going on around her, and requires constant care. People such as that belong in institutions. That's why we pay taxes, so that there will be places for people like that."

Jerry's mother was about to explode, and Jerry edged over to a far corner of the parlor so that he wouldn't get in the way of the fireworks. "Ivy's not helpless. She can dress and feed herself. I've watched her do it." Jerry's mother said, as loudly as she could without shouting.

“Yes, and after she does what any six year old can do, she sits in her rocking chair and stares out at nothing for the rest of the day,” Grandmother answered.

“Ginnie thinks Ivy will eventually emerge from this state she’s in, if she's allowed to exist in a warm environment.”

“And you think this is a warm environment?” Grandmother’s voice was now louder than her daughter's. “How long has it been since you and Eric have had a discussion lasting longer than ten words?”

“You leave my husband out of this,” Jerry's mother said, “This is about my helping out a dear friend and her daughter, and is none of your business at all...”

Jerry stood watching and listening as the two women argued, feeling like a stain on the wall paper. Shortly the women agreed to disagree. Grandmother left, saying she didn’t wish to be on hand when Ginnie and Ivy Barnes arrived. Mother went to check her appearance in a mirror, leaving Jerry alone in the parlor. “I got an ‘A’ on my English paper,” Jerry announced, though there was no one to hear him.

He sat in a crushed velvet chair to wait for the company to arrive, his mind returning to thoughts of Mae.

TWO

"I always thought you rich people had butlers to help haul in the luggage," Ginnie Barnes said, as she pulled the first of many well-worn suitcases from the trunk of her car.

"Not anymore," Jerry said, taking the bag from Mrs. Barnes. "The only things we have in the way of servants are a team of house cleaners who come in several times a week to scrub the old place over and trim the hedges."

"You're forgetting Mrs. Thompson, dear," Mrs. Sebastian said.

"Oh, yeah," Jerry said. "She's our cook. She's more like family than a servant, though."

"Penelope," Mrs. Barnes said, "I had no idea of how good looking a man your son has grown into. He's tall, dark and so, so handsome, just like his father."

Jerry walked into the house with Mrs. Barnes' bag. He didn't mind helping bring in the luggage, but he drew the line at being embarrassed. He returned for more bags, and when all the bags and suit containers had been brought in, only one chore remained, and that was taking Ivy out of the car and bringing her into the house. She had been sitting in the front seat of the Barnes's Ford the entire time, and even her own mother had been acting as if her slumped figure wasn't really there.

"She's not very good about walking on her own in strange places," Mrs. Barnes said as she swung open the door of the aging Ford. "We're going to have to help her." Clutching Ivy by the hand, Mrs. Barnes pulled her out of the car. Then she motioned for Jerry to come around to one side of Ivy, and together they walked her up into the house. Physically Ivy looked normal, perhaps even a little better than normal. Her California blonde hair was trimmed off at her ears, and Jerry couldn't help imagining how terrific it would look if her hair was shoulder length. He realized, though, that long hair takes a lot of time to take care of, particularly when the owner of the hair is unable to take care of it herself. Ivy's face was perfectly constructed, as was her body, and Jerry couldn't help but think what a waste it was that such beauty had been given to a girl who would never be able to use it. Mrs. Barnes and Jerry led Ivy into the parlor and over to the crushed velvet chair Jerry had been sitting in earlier. As they tried to get her to sit down in the chair, though, her previously limp body tightened. "She has problems sitting in anything but her rocking chair," Mrs. Barnes explained. "It's okay, Ivy," she said to her daughter as she gently pushed her into a sitting position. "We'll have your rocking chair for you as soon as possible." The tone in Mrs. Barnes' voice was that of somebody speaking to a baby, and despite Ivy's condition Jerry thought that tone an insulting one to use on anyone close to his own age. But he figured Mrs. Barnes knew best. He looked at Ivy as she sat uneasily in the crushed velvet chair, and for the first time got a clear view of her crystal blue eyes. But they were like the eyes of a dead person, dull and unlit. "Jerry," Mrs. Barnes said, "would you mind helping get her rocking chair out of the back of our car? Ivy's lost without it, and—" Mrs. Barnes stopped in the middle of her sentence and looked down with dismay at Ivy, who had thrown up all over the crushed velvet chair.

"I'll go get that chair right now," Jerry said, quickly making his way out of the parlor.

"I'm so sorry, Penelope," he heard Mrs. Barnes tell Mother after he was in the hallway,

"It's okay," Mother answered, though Jerry could hear the anguish in her voice.

As Jerry walked outside to retrieve the rocking chair, his heart was heavy with sadness over the impression Ivy had just given, because this wasn't the first time he'd met her. But the first and last time before this had been the day he'd turned six, when Ivy was five. Mother threw a big birthday party for Jerry, and all the local children were invited. Mr. and Mrs. Barnes happened to be in town on a business trip, and Mother invited them to the party as well. Ivy was a bit strange then, too, but not any stranger than all little girls seem to be to a six-year-old boy. Ivy had taken one look at Jerry, smiled an enormous smile, and didn't leave him alone the rest of the day. Everywhere he went, she followed, and the other kids started calling her 'Jerry's shadow'. Usually this sort of thing would have really bugged Jerry, especially on his birthday. But though he pretended not to like having her follow him around, since a boy does have his reputation to maintain, he could still recall secretly liking having her around. For a girl, she seemed okay to him. He always remembered how Ivy had cried when it came time for the Barnes's to go. "But I love him, mommy," she had said, pointing at Jerry. Mr. Barnes managed to calm his daughter down by promising they'd be back for another visit in a year. Jerry remembered how long Ivy had waved at him as she and her parents drove off to the airport to return to the east coast. He also remembered all too well the reason they didn't come back for another visit a year later. Mother had said at the time that was a miracle Ivy didn’t die like her father did in the burning remains of their wrecked car. Mr. Barnes had taken Ivy out for ice cream, and a drunken driver had slammed his car head-on into theirs. Rescue workers found Ivy covered in her father’s blood, still holding on to his dead hand. Only she wasn’t crying. She wasn’t doing anything at all. And hadn’t done much of anything since. And now, having seen her himself, Jerry was sure there really hadn’t been a miracle at all, Ivy had died along with her father. She’d simply forgotten to tell her body. Jerry looked at how the rocking chair had been positioned on the back seat of the Ford. Though the chair was tiny, it still filled up a large part of the equally small back seat of the car. As he began to carefully maneuver it out of the back seat, he tried to chase the sad thoughts out of his head and replace them with new thoughts of Mae, but it wasn't as easy as it had been earlier.

THREE

The Barnes women spent a quiet first evening in the Sebastian home. Mrs. Barnes concentrated on unpacking. Ivy sat in her rocking chair, not concentrating on anything at all.

Jerry was in his room, sitting at his desk. Plenty of trigonometry homework stared up at him, but he wasn't staring back. He wasn't thinking about Mae, of course. He was dreaming about her. He didn't know exactly why he was so crazy about her in particular. He could have virtually any girl in high school he wanted, in fact almost every one at one time or another had let him know it. Jerry long ago had found out that he was the boy the girls like to dream and talk about in the girls' locker room. The only girl who played hard to get was Mae, and this, Jerry realized, could be the reason he liked her.

At breakfast the next morning, the center of interest was naturally Ivy. What sort of table manners would she have? Mrs. Barnes led her to the table and helped her sit down. "Mrs. Thompson," Mother said to the cook as soon as Ivy was seated, "please get Ivy some breakfast."

"What does she eat?" Mrs. Thompson asked. Being more prim and proper than any member of the Sebastian family, Mrs. Thompson seemed miffed that no one had already told her what to prepare for Ivy.

"Scrambled eggs are fine," Mrs. Barnes said.

"We'll all have scrambled eggs," Mother added.

"Would you like me to give you a hand?" Mrs. Barnes asked.

Mrs. Thompson gave Mrs. Barnes a "how dare you" glance. "That's all right, ma'am," she said, "I've been preparing scrambled eggs for forty years now, and I don't think I've forgotten how since yesterday." Mrs. Thompson marched into the kitchen, and the rest of them sat around the dining table waiting for their grub.

Father, as usual, was heavily involved in reading the business section of the New York Times. Nothing normally could distract him from reading his paper at the breakfast table. Jerry could start choking and Father would probably only look away from the paper long enough to suggest calling an ambulance. Jerry looked at Ivy, sitting expressionless across from him, and thought it would be easier to have a conversation with her than it would be with his father. Mrs. Thompson entered with a large platter full of scrambled eggs and set it down in the center of the table. "Anybody need refills?" she asked.

"I need more orange juice," Jerry said.

"Coffee, please," Father said, not looking up from his newspaper.

Mrs. Thompson turned and passed through the swinging doors which led to the kitchen, returning moments later carrying a pitcher of orange juice in one hand and a carafe of coffee in the other. Her years of experience showed as she simultaneously filled both Jerry's and Mr. Sebastian's cups. Jerry was waiting for the day she would goof and pour coffee in his orange juice glass, but so far Mrs. Thompson had been perfect. She then started scooping up the eggs and placing equal helpings of them on everyone's plates. But no one started eating except Mrs. Barnes. Instead they watched Ivy slowly grab hold of her fork. Jerry noticed that even Father had slightly lowered his newspaper to spy on the proceedings. "Go on, Ivy honey," Mrs. Barnes said softly, "show everybody that you can feed yourself." Ivy proceeded to start eating just like a normal person, and quickly the level of interest evaporated, and it seemed like just an ordinary breakfast.

Ivy, naturally, didn't accompany Jerry to school. As he left, Ivy was in her rocking chair, and Mrs. Barnes was reading to her. Mrs. Barnes said she'd been reading to Ivy since soon after the accident, and that she was convinced Ivy was listening and learning from the books. Jerry couldn't help but wonder just how much Ivy really could have possibly learned in her state. He parked the Mustang in the student parking lot and was closing the car door when he noticed Mae walking down the sidewalk. She paused and looked at him briefly without saying hello before continuing. Jerry stood staring at her as she walked into the school building. "Nice weather we're having," Sam Figouri said, as he came up next to Jerry, "it gives you a great view." Sam started to pant. Jerry felt like telling Sam to go back to the sewer he'd crawled out from. It was one thing if he leered at Mae; after all, he wanted to be her guy. It was entirely wrong for Sam to do so, however, because all Sam wanted to do was leer and slobber at her, and he probably wouldn't know what to do if she asked him to go with her.

But instead of giving Sam a lesson in ethics, which wouldn't be very cool, Jerry simply agreed with him. "Yeah, terrific view," he mumbled.

"All right if I come over tonight?" Sam asked, "It's about time I finally beat you."

Sam loved to come and shoot pool in the Sebastian game room. Jerry didn't love it as much because he always beat Sam, who would then make stupid excuses about not being lucky enough to own his own pool table. Despite this, Jerry was about to extend the usual invitation to Sam when a warning alarm flashed across his brain. What would Sam think about Ivy? Not that he necessarily cared what Sam Figouri thought about anything, but Sam did have a big mouth and surely the entire school would know Jerry had a freak living in his house. The house was big enough that Sam might not see Ivy, but Jerry couldn't afford to take the chance. "Sorry, it can't be tonight," he said.

"You got something else planned?" Sam asked, trying but failing to hide his disappointment.

"Yeah," Jerry answered, unable to think of exactly what else he had planned. The five minute warning bell rang, forcing Jerry and Sam to make their way to class. All the way to Advanced Biology, and for the rest of the day, Jerry couldn't help but feel like a rat. But being a popular rat was better than being an unpopular saint.

FOUR

Jerry spent the rest of the school day alternating between two thoughts: how much he liked Mae; and how his house would now have to off limits to anybody he knew. The first thought filled him with pleasure, the second made him sick. One of the reasons people liked him was because of the house, with its fancy furniture and well equipped game room. But he really didn't have much choice. By sixth period, however, Jerry's mind was on nothing but basketball. It may have just been P.E., but when it came to hoops there was only one way for Jerry to go, and that was all out. Or as all out as possible when half the teams are composed of girls. Some of the guys didn't care about getting rough with the girls as a part of the competition, but the thought always made Jerry feel uneasy. Some of the girls weren't at all athletic, and the only reason they were on the same floor with the boys was because of some sort of federal law that said they had to be. They could be hurt very easily, Jerry felt, and that just wasn't fair because they didn't ask to be on the court in the first place.

Despite Jerry's leadership, his team was losing by a point when he noticed it was just about time to head for the showers. His side had possession of the ball, however, and with any luck they'd be able to quickly score two points before the coach blew the shower whistle. Lucy Morgan in-bounded the ball to Jerry, and he dribbled the ball past one defender and was going in for a quick lay-up when suddenly Nancy Lewis jumped into his path. He tried to veer around her, but he lost his balance and felt his leg crumple underneath him. The game stopped and everybody circled around Jerry, who, though he was in great pain as he lay flat on the floor, did his best to be brave. "I guess my leg's broken, coach," Jerry said to Coach Jackson, who was kneeling down looking at Jerry's leg.

"No, you've only got a dislocated knee, nothing to worry about, son," the coach said, in a calm voice.

"Then why is that bone sticking out?" Jerry asked, before losing consciousness.

When Jerry woke up, not only was he in the hospital, but a nurse was sitting on his bedside, watching the television which hung from the ceiling in a corner of the room. "Oh, you're awake," she said when she noticed him stirring; "I just love this show, don't you?" Jerry tried to answer, but couldn't because his throat was groggy and he didn't know what show it was she was watching. "Don't try to speak, darling, you've been through a lot today," she said. "Perhaps you're wondering why I'm sitting here on your bed." Jerry nodded his head and the nurse continued. "You see, after you came out of surgery you were cranky, and the orderlies had a devil of a time keeping you from throwing them against the wall as they tried to restrain you from moving about." Jerry aimed his sleepy eyes toward his legs, but could only actually see one of them. The other one was encased from toe to thigh in a plaster east. Immediately Jerry realized his basketball season was over before it had even started. "One RN was shoved to the floor by you," the nurse continued, "I've always found that the gentle approach is best when dealing with patients who are waking up after surgery. All those big orderlies couldn't keep you from tossing and turning, and just my sitting on your bedside, occasionally stroking your hair, kept you calm."

Jerry looked through his sleep filled eyes around the hospital room, to see if Mother or Father had bothered to show up. But other than the nurse, there wasn't anyone else in the room. "Does my family know I'm here?" he asked, with a voice which sounded like only half the vocal cords were awake.

"Oh, yes, they knew right away. I've always felt the best place for a kid to get hurt is at school, because they immediately know how to get in touch with the parents." The nurse smiled at Jerry, however, the smile quickly dissolved as she remembered something. "Oh, you have someone waiting to see you," she said, before getting up off the bed and racing out into the hallway. She returned a few seconds later, followed by Mrs. Thompson.

"Jerry, it's good to see you awake," the cook said, with her knitting in her hands and a worried look carved on her face. "You were in that operating room a long time."

Jerry looked at the nurse quizzically, until now he'd been too groggy to ask questions about how bad his leg was. "You were in surgery four hours," said the nurse. "The doctor said he was able to piece your leg together well. He'll come by during rounds tomorrow to fill you in more."

"Did Mother come by?" Jerry asked Mrs. Thompson, knowing full well that Father wouldn't have bothered.

"She was in the middle of chairing the weekly historical society meeting, so she sent me."

It figured, Jerry thought. He could be near death and his parents' social commitments would still come first. Though he didn't want to be rude, he started feeling groggy again, and before he could say anything else he was asleep once more. When he awoke it was quite apparent he'd been conked out for a while, because the nurse and Mrs. Thompson were both gone, the TV was turned off, and bright sunlight had replaced the darkness which now draped the corners of the room. A man in a white coat was staring down at him.

"Hello I'm Dr. Argan," the man said. "I'm the guy who put your leg back together."

"How bad is it?" Jerry asked, though he wasn't sure he really wanted to know.

"It'll be as good as new in about six months."

"Oh," Jerry groaned, as he envisioned a basketball court without him for six months. "How long will I have to stay here?"

"About three hours more," Dr. Argan said. "I spoke with your mother on the phone and she feels that though you won't be able to go to school for the next two weeks, there's no reason why you can't get the same care at home that you would here. And, knowing your family, I would think you'd probably get even better care at home."

Fine, Jerry thought, not only was he not going to be able to play hoops for six months, but he had to also listen to this quack make cracks about him being rich. "Anything else I should know about my leg?" he asked, since he still knew next to nothing about how bad it actually was.

"Not really, except that you're not going to be very mobile with that particular cast on. Of course, that's on purpose, to give the bones a chance to start knitting together. In a couple of weeks, when you're ready to return to school, we'll fix you up with a smaller cast, but until then you're not going to be able to do much other than catch up on your television viewing."

Mrs. Thompson appeared a couple of hours later to drive Jerry home. She even brought a gift from Mother and Father. It was a wheelchair. “We’ve rented it for few weeks to help you get around the house,” Mrs. Thompson said. As an orderly wheeled Jerry out of the hospital, Jerry couldn’t help but feel sorry for himself. Not only was basketball out of the question, but so was driving his Mustang, or any car with a clutch. And he didn’t know how he was going to keep all the friends who would probably come by to see him from seeing Ivy as well.

FIVE

Unable to leave home, Jerry found himself assigned the task of being constant company for Ivy. Mrs. Barnes had an assortment of books she liked to read to Ivy. She saw no reason why her daughter couldn't learn by listening. Jerry wasn't convinced that reading to Ivy would do anything more than take time away from his own studies, but he agreed to do it, if only for that reason. Jerry spent forty-five minutes dutifully attending to his studies before deciding he wasn't in the right kind of mood for advancing his education. Slapping shut his copy of Western Civilization, he looked over at Ivy. She was still gently rocking in her chair, serenely in her own world. He wondered what went on in her mind. Surely something had to be happening inside her head. But judging from her expressionless glacier face it was hard to think that she still had feelings. Putting his history book back on top of his pile of books, Jerry examined the ones in Ivy's stack. The titles included The Works of Shakespeare, Little House on the Prairie, and the New American Bible. Nothing that Jerry exactly felt like reading aloud. But he'd promised Mrs. Barnes he would read to Ivy from these books, so, sighing, he reached for the Shakespeare. Pushing his wheelchair over so he was by Ivy's side, he opened the thick book and read the first thing his eyes landed on. "Launce, away, away, aboard! Thy master is shipped, and thou art to post after with oars." Just as quickly as he had opened the book, he closed it. It was hard to see how this could possibly help Ivy, and anyway, how would Mrs. Barnes ever know that he hadn't read it to Ivy? Ivy certainly wouldn't tell. So instead he found a Sidney Sheldon novel and spent the rest of the day reading that to Ivy.

Mrs. Barnes returned around four, and Jerry quickly hid the Sidney Sheldon in the bookcase just before she came into the study. Jerry was impressed at how Mrs. Barnes rushed over to Ivy. If he had been chained to her for all those years, he wouldn't have been in such a hurry to end his first day of freedom. "How's my girl been?" She asked, placing a kiss on Ivy's frozen face. "I hope you didn't miss me very much today." Suddenly the smile on Mrs. Barnes' face disappeared and she turned to Jerry glaring. "You didn't read to her from any of her books, did you?"

Jerry was taken too much by surprise to lie. "How'd you know?" he asked, embarrassment flavoring his words.

"Ivy told me," she said. "I thought you promised to read to her."

"I did read to her," Jerry insisted.

"What did you read to her?"

Reaching to the bookcase, Jerry retrieved the Sidney Sheldon. "I read her this."

"That sort of writing doesn't help anybody," Mrs. Barnes said. "I think if you promise to do something, you should do it. You've disappointed me greatly." Mrs. Barnes left the room in a huff, leaving Jerry alone with Ivy.

Jerry looked into Ivy's blank face. It didn't seem possible that this girl could have told on him, Mrs. Barnes must have seen him hiding the book. "I'm sorry," he told Ivy, just in case. To his amazement, Ivy smiled brightly back at him.

SIX

Ivy's smile had quickly disappeared, but it didn't disappear fast enough to keep Jerry from thinking about it that entire evening. He ate a quiet dinner, so quiet that Mother made a joke about him making less noise than Ivy. Mrs. Barnes didn't think much of the joke, and Mother had to spend the rest of the meal apologizing. Jerry lay awake in bed that night and wondered why it seemed that every time he thought he had life all figured out, something would happen, such as Ivy smiling, which would confuse him all over again. He kept trying to convince himself that Ivy's smile was some kind of involuntary reaction, like how babies look as if they're smiling when they really only have gas. But he couldn't do it, her smile was as real and genuine as anybody else's, and nothing he could think of would make him believe otherwise.

The next morning Mrs. Barnes told Jerry that he didn't have to read to Ivy if he didn't really want to, but Jerry said he did want to. Mrs. Barnes looked surprised at the change in Jerry's attitude, but didn't say anything about it. Mrs. Barnes left, and everything was the same as it had been the day before, except that the day before Jerry had believed he was being left alone, and today he knew he had company. He looked at Ivy as she sat placidly in her rocking chair, and felt like screaming at her to snap out of it, because he was on to her and did not want to put up with the silent treatment any longer. However, deciding that yelling only works in baseball; he instead started reading her books to her.

At first it wasn't very much fun, but slowly Jerry began to notice that Ivy was listening carefully to every word he read. He wasn't sure exactly how he knew this, and most people would think there been little change at all in her icy blank face. But Jerry had spent enough time with Ivy to notice that her eyes did not remain the same. They changed with everything that was said. Jerry felt like he was losing his mind, if a few days ago someone had told him he would he so concerned about somebody like Ivy, he probably would have laughed before slugging that person down the most convenient staircase. Now it was different, and he wasn't entirely sure why. He reached down into the magazine holder of his wheelchair and pulled out the remains of an old wire coat hanger, which he now found himself using more and more often to reach the itches underneath his cast. In the middle of scratching his leg, he glanced up in time to see Ivy smiling. "Oh, so you think it's funny that I'm forced to scratch my leg this way," he said to her teasingly. Her smile grew larger, the aware gleam in her eyes shone brighter. She had understood what he had said, and was reacting to it as a normal girl would. Leaving the coat hanger wire he raised his hand and reached over to squeeze one of Ivy's hands in congratulation, but no sooner had he grasped her hand than the signs of awareness vanished from her face, and she was like a vegetable once more. "Don't worry, Ivy," Jerry said softly, "Someday you're going to come out to visit me and I'll make sure you don't go back."

SEVEN

The study of the Sebastian home was sedately lit in the light of a mid-October afternoon. Outside, stormy skies readied themselves for another attack, there wasn't going to be an Indian summer this year. Jerry had been left to study and watch Ivy, just as he had for the last couple of weeks since returning from the hospital. But there weren't any lights on in the study because Jerry was again ignoring his homework to talk with Ivy.

"I don't know about you, but I think the Trailblazers have a long way to go before they can even hope to win it all," Jerry said to Ivy. She gave no response, maintaining her usual blank stare. "I'm sorry," Jerry said, "I should have known you don't care for sports." Jerry had been talking to Ivy about anything that came into his mind for days now, hoping to find something that would cause a reaction in her. Only rarely did any reaction surface on her face, just enough to keep Jerry talking. Jerry was convinced that his non-stop talking would eventually help Ivy come out of her shell. In any case, the talks were helping him, since he could talk with Ivy about things he couldn't discuss with anyone else.

"Sometimes I wonder if I really have a chance with Mae," he said, "I mean, she could probably choose from any guy she wants, and I really don't know if I'm one of the guys she wants."

"I just love the way you two have become friends," Mrs. Barnes said, walking into the study.

"How long have you been home?" Jerry asked. He hated to think that she had overheard him getting sappy about Mae.

"I just got here," Mrs. Barnes answered, though she looked as if she was smothering a smile. "You could use a little more light in here," she said, walking over to a corner lamp and switching it on. "There, that's better."

"I think I like this room better when it's dark," Jerry said.

"I didn't realize you were so gloomy," Mrs. Barnes said.

"I'm not. I just think this study looks better when filled with dark spaces and shadows."

Mrs. Barnes reached over and switched the lamp back off. "You know, you're right," she said, glancing around the darkened room. "Having the lights off does make this study look nicely Victorian."

"I was thinking of those old black and white movies they used to show on television, before they found out how to color them."

Mrs. Barnes took another glance around the room. "You're right," she said, "I feel as if Humphrey Bogart will emerge from the shadows any moment now. I did not know you liked old movies, I've always heard you were into sports."

"There are a lot of things my parents wouldn't ever tell you about me, because they don't know themselves."

"They've always been busy people."

"Busy with everything but me."

Mrs. Barnes shook her head sadly. "Isn't it funny? I'd do almost anything in order to listen to Ivy tell me about her problems, and most parents whose kids are okay spend all their time avoiding any sort of real conversation with them."

"Tell me about it," Jerry said, thinking about his relationship with his own parents.

"By the way, I have a favor to ask you," Mrs. Barnes said, as the mood in the room suddenly shifted to a less personal one. "I know you've been good about staying with Ivy during the days since you broke your leg, and I was wondering if you'd mind staying with her this Friday night. I've been invited to a party."

"Of course I'll stay with her," Jerry answered, as he looked over at Ivy. She was sitting as still as she usually did, only now with the smallest trace of a smile on her lips. "I couldn't think of a better friend to spend a Friday evening with."

"You know, Jerry, I wish every high school kid was as nice as you," Mrs. Barnes said, giving Jerry a peck on the cheek. Jerry watched as she pushed Ivy in her wheelchair out of the study, and a strange emotion welled up inside him. In his life he'd been called many things by many people, but this was the first time he could remember someone telling him he was nice.

EIGHT

It was the late afternoon of the next day, and Jerry and Ivy were as usual in the study when Mrs. Thompson came in. "You have visitors," she announced, as several people followed her into the room. Sam Figouri and Chuck Williams were the first two visitors, but it was the third one who made Jerry's mouth drop open. Mae

Ann Reynolds' beauty had only grown greater in the weeks since Jerry had last seen her.

"Jerry, you never told me you lived in such a nice house," Mae Ann said, spinning around in a graceful, ballet flourish in order to see all of the elegant surroundings.

"It's just where we've always lived," Jerry said, unsuccessfully trying to hide his embarrassment.

"Jerry's family is rich," Sam said. "There's nothing his family won't give him."

"That's not entirely true," Jerry protested.

"You have to admit they give you a whole lot," Chuck said. "I once heard of a rich family in Mississippi who kept their only son chained in their basement..."

"Chuck Williams," Mae Ann said, "If you're about to tell us another one of your gross stories, don't." Her voice rose on don't, and Chuck's face had the look of a puppy about to be swatted on the nose with a newspaper. Mae Ann walked away from Sam and Chuck and breezed up to Ivy. "You must be that weird girl I've heard about," she said to Ivy's blank gaze. "I just can't see how you've survived the last couple of weeks, Jerry."

"What do you mean?" Jerry asked, though he already knew what direction Mae Ann was heading in.

"I mean, I couldn't stand a single day of being chained to a freak like this."

Jerry felt anger unlike any he'd ever experienced. He'd always been very good about controlling his moments of anger, as well as any of his real feelings, because having friends was important to him. But the anger he now felt couldn't be controlled, because Ivy meant more to him than his friends. "Get out of here," he screamed. The two boys immediately scrambled out the door. But Mae Ann stood staring at Jerry with a look of disbelief. "I said get out of my house now." Mae Ann, looking like she was going to weep, turned and ran out. Jerry looked over at Ivy. And she gave him the brightest smile he'd ever seen.

Then she said something. Her voice was rough from disuse, however, and he couldn't understand her. He leaned in closer, and when she spoke again he did understand. "I love you, Jerry," Ivy said.

A Touching Moment

1

March, 1992

"Claire, you need to learn what it means to be a girl."

"But, Josalyn, I am a girl."

"That's a lie."

"Huh?"

An awkward silence happened as the two girls walked under an overcast Oregon sky. “What I mean,” Josalyn finally said, “is your idea of what it means to be a girl is just a big lie created by men to enslave women.” Even though Josalyn Braden thought a person should control his or her anger, she was having an awful time controlling hers. And though she was against using violence, right now she wanted to wring Claire Thompson’s neck. “Look, Claire, I’ve talked until my lungs are about to collapse, what more can I say to make you get it?”

“Get what?” Claire asked, edging her way down the sidewalk.

“That’s the point. You just don’t get it. You need to go through your closet, and toss out everything pink. Why do you have so many pink clothes?”

“Uh, because I’m a girl?”

“Claire, you’re not a girl, you’re a sexual stereotype.”

“A what?” Claire asked, tears forming in her eyes. “I was being your friend because I felt sorry for you, but if you’re going to call me dirty names, I don’t think

I can be friends with you any longer." Claire dashed off down the sidewalk.

"Claire, wait!" But Claire kept running. It was just as well, Josalyn thought. Claire was unlikely to catch on about how evil men were if she didn't even know what stereotype meant. And all she wanted to do was look at clothes. That's what they had spent the morning doing. And Claire didn't want to look at jeans and T-shirts. She liked looking at dresses. And pink clothes. Josalyn couldn't understand why so many women felt they had to dress to please men. Everything that's wrong with this world is men's fault. They're all so stupid. And they always do wrong. Josalyn's eyes grew big. She wished Claire hadn't run off, because she could have witnessed a man doing evil. He was getting some money out of the automated teller. But he had parked his car in the handicapped space. Like most men, he was taking unfair advantage. What if a disabled person needed that space right now? What he's doing is downright criminal, Josalyn thought, as she seethed with anger. It probably wasn't even his own account that he was getting money from. He probably had stolen some poor woman's bank card. Her face red with anger, Josalyn ran to the man. "You should be ashamed," she said. The man calmly listened as Josalyn told him off, then turned to reveal what Josalyn had not seen from the sidewalk. He was missing a leg. Using a single crutch on his legless side, the man went back to his car. Josalyn, looking as if her face would slide off her head, rushed to open the man's car door. The man put his crutch into the car, and just before getting in himself, he smiled at Josalyn and patted her on the head. This brought back her anger. You'd think being physically challenged would have made him more sensitive, she thought, as she walked home. After all, thirteen is too old to be patted on the head.

2

Josalyn saw the ambulance leave the driveway of the house she shared with her mother and grandmother, but instead of being alarmed, she was sad. It meant HE was here. Gram had been a nurse for many years before retiring recently. But no sooner had she retired than she heard about a man who had been totally paralyzed in a car accident, to the point of barely being able to breathe. The man had little money, other than government help, and was having a hard time finding a place that could take care of his special needs on his limited funds. Gram volunteered to take him into her home. Josalyn would normally think it a wonderful thing for Gram to do, except for two things. The first thing was that this man had been a Christian evangelist. A full-fledged member of the religious right, the group most opposed to what Josalyn believed in. But the second, and most important reason she didn't want this guy moving in was that he had to take away her room. There was no choice about it, Josalyn's big, wonderful room, her home for as long as she wanted to remember, was the only one on the first story of their house. And therefore, the only one the man could be easily moved into. So while workers had built wheelchair ramps on the front and back stoops of their old house, Josalyn had glumly hauled everything she owned upstairs, to the tiny room at the top of the stairs. Josalyn walked into the house, and heard the sounds of her mother and Gram coming from her old room. "Mom, I'm home," she yelled, as she started up the stairs.

"Josalyn, come and meet our new guest," Gram called out. Josalyn kept going up the stairs. "Right now, young lady." Turning around, Josalyn went up to the door of her old room, inhaled deeply, and went in. Her room was now totally different. Machines were everywhere. A special hospital bed was in the center. And in the bed was Gram's patient.

"Mr. Minlow, this is my daughter, Josalyn," Josalyn's mother said.

"Hi," Josalyn said. He was younger than she thought. And what she noticed most of all was the huge smile on his face. She tried to think about the oxygen mask on his face, or how his body lay motionless beneath the covers. But though she prided herself on being a thinker, there were moments were she couldn't control her feelings, and this was one. This was her room, and he had no right to be happy about taking it from her.

"I'm happy to meet you, Josalyn," the man said, in a husky whisper.

"You should be happy," Josalyn snapped. "You've got the best room in the house." Then, before anyone could see her cry, she sprinted out the door and up the stairs to her new room, where she buried her head in her pillow. A few minutes later, her mother stuck her head in the door.

"Apologize," she said, in a low, angry tone. "The only way you're going to leave this room, or have dinner, is if you first go to Mr. Minlow's room and ask him to forgive you."

"But, Mother, he's in my room. He should apologize to me."

"I don't know how I came to have such a spoiled, selfish daughter. Well, if you get hungry, you know what you have to do." Her mother closed the door as she left, and Josalyn was full of guilt. Mother was right. The way Josalyn had just treated Mr. Minlow went against all her principles. He may be a member of the religious right, but he also was physically challenged. And, for all she knew, Mr. Minlow's problems may have caused him to change his hate-filled beliefs. After grabbing a tissue to dry her face, she crept back down the stairs, to her old room. Mother saw her and said, "Well, Mr. Minlow, I believe Josalyn has something to say to you."

Josalyn stepped closer to the bed. "I'm sorry for the way I acted, Mr. Minlow."

"No reason to be sorry, honey," he said, in his husky whisper.

"You're not angry?"

"Of course not. No little girl likes to give up her special bedroom."

"Little girl?" Josalyn asked, trying to hold her temper.

"I mean, little boys can camp out just about anywhere, but once a little girl has her room decorated the way she likes it, it's tough for her to move to another room."

"Listen," Josalyn snapped.

"Josalyn...." warned her mother, but it was too late.

"I'm sorry about what's happened to you, but you need to be set straight about some things. First, I'm not a child. I'm a young person. And I don't appreciate your assuming I'm a certain way just because I'm a woman, you, you, sexist Christian bigot!" Josalyn again ran back to her new room, once again buried her head in her pillow. But this time, her mother waited before coming to see her. Josalyn knew this meant she was really angry. Her policy when really angry was to go cool off somewhere before giving out punishment.

"You're lucky I waited a half hour," her mother said when she finally came through the door. "Because I've never wanted to spank you more than I did a few minutes ago. Instead I've decided on a different punishment for you."

"But Mother, he called me a child."

"You are a child. And for the next month, you are to come straight home from school every day and spend an hour visiting with Mr. Minlow."

"You've got to be kidding."

"No. Mr. Minlow said the toughest thing he faces isn't his body condition, but loneliness. I asked him whether he would like having you spend some detention time with him, and he said sure. After how you've treated him, I think that's really special."

"But I can't stand him, Mother."

"You'd better learn. If you can't say something nice, don't say anything. But you will be there every school-day for one hour, giving that poor man someone to talk with. And for every time you can't control the urge to hurl an insult at him, I will add an extra day to your punishment. Do you understand?"

"Yes," Josalyn said gloomily. "Is it still possible to get a spanking instead?"

3

"You're late, Josalyn," Gram said, as Josalyn dragged herself through the front door.

"I'm sorry, Gram. I had to go explain to Ms. Greer why I wouldn't be able to help with the Environment Club's after school paper drive."

"Well, I'll let it pass this time. But your mother said that you were to have an extra day added every time you're late. You had better go in. "He's waiting for you."

Josalyn, still carrying her backpack, walked slowly into her old room. Mr. Minlow saw her and smiled. "Good to see you again, Miss Josalyn," he said, in a good-natured voice that was not as much a whisper as before.

"What's with this Miss Josalyn junk? Why don't you just call me Josalyn?"

"Don't you like the dignified sound of it? I do."

"At least you could use Ms., Mr. Minlow," Josalyn said.

"Oh," Mr. Minlow said. "Well, it's still good to see you again."

"Look, I'm here because I have no choice. I'm not of legal age, and that means I'm open to any sort of abuse that my mother chooses to give me, just because society labels me a child. There's nothing I have to say to you. But if you want to talk, go right ahead, and I'll sit here and pretend to listen." Josalyn sat on the nurse's bedside chair. Glaring up at Mr. Minlow, she saw that his smile had not faded one bit. The man had to be totally loony.

"Well, Ms. Josalyn, I realize we don't have anything to talk about, and judging from your behavior the other day, I can see you have a great deal to learn."

"I get good grades."

"I'm sure you do. So it should be easy for you to learn the content of this book." He nodded his head toward the little pink book on the dresser. "I'm feeling lazy right now, so could you please go pick it up for me."

Josalyn stood, picked up the book and read the title aloud. "Smiles and Party Manners." The cover was illustrated with a drawing of a smiling little girl wearing an old-fashioned party dress. She was even wearing little white gloves. Josalyn opened it and saw it was printed in 1964. "What, do you collect ancient, out of date books from the Stone Age," she said, laughing.

"I'm glad I found a way to make you laugh. But good manners never go out of date, though they seem to be out of style, because there haven't been many good books on them since the late sixties."

"What's the point?"

"The point is that you need to learn some manners, young lady."

"You're crazier than I thought." Josalyn was about to call him more names, but controlled herself. "I mean, nobody follows this sort of junk any longer. It just encourages class distinctions and sexism."

"Who was the fool who told you that?"

Josalyn was sure she felt steam coming from her ears. "Ms. Greer, my art teacher."

"Since when is being kind and polite to others wrong? I can see you have more to learn than I thought." Mr. Minlow's smile still hadn't changed one bit. "For that reason you are to memorize this book completely."

"You've got to be kidding."

"You will be able to repeat back to me anything I ask you to, and I will then expect you to practice what you have learned and report back to me about it."

"And what if I don't?"

"Then I won't cut your time with me in half."

"What?"

"You heard me. If you learn that book well enough to recite it by heart, then instead of being stuck with me for a month, you'll be set loose on the world again in two weeks."

"You're speaking better today than the other day."

"I'm not tired out from moving. And don't try to wiggle off the subject. Will you learn what's in that book?"

Josalyn swallowed hard. If she could cut her punishment in half, she could still help with the paper drive. And it was a thin little kid's book. "I hope you don't expect me to actually live by these rules."

"That's up to you. I just think you should know them."

"Okay if I sit down and start memorizing it now?"

"Why don't you open it to the first chapter?" Josalyn opened the slender book to the front. "Read the little paragraph titled: Why a Miss."

"But."

"Read."

"Why a Miss?" Josalyn looked away from the page. "Why this book?" she asked.

"Read."

"Everybody knows that single girls are Misses and that married ladies are Mrs.... But what if you don't know whether a lady is married or not? Use Miss. Miss is also used to address women who choose to keep their maiden names, or even the rare married woman who doesn't want people to know her marriage status. When there's any doubt, you can't miss by using Miss." Josalyn looked at Mr. Minlow. "There, I've read it."

"What do you think of that?"

"Were women allowed to keep their maiden names way back then?"

"Well, it's true that most women did not keep their maiden names, but it's always been a woman's choice. What do think of the word Miss, judging from what you've read there?"

"It makes it sound like it was used the way Ms. is now. I thought it only meant that a woman was unmarried."

"That's what she wants you to think."

"Who's that?"

"The woman who invented the word Ms. When you go around fixing things that work just fine, you have to pretend they don't."

"That's crazy. Why would someone want to fix something that wasn't a problem?"

"You're right, it is crazy. Especially when Miss sounds so much better than Mizzz...."

"Why do you know this book so well?"

"This isn't the first time I've had a young lady study it," he said, nodding his head toward the picture frame on the bureau. The photograph was of him and the family who had died in the car accident. A wife with an elaborate hairdo, and two young daughters. All with smiles too big to be real. Suddenly, Josalyn felt terrible about the way she'd been treating Mr. Minlow. He may be a jerk, but even jerks don't deserve what had happened to him.

"It's okay." Josalyn said softly.

"What's okay?"

"If it makes you feel good to call me Miss, go ahead. Just don't spread it around."

"Don't worry, Miss Josalyn, it won't leave this room."

4

Josalyn carried the book of manners to school with her the next day, thinking the sooner she learned it, the better. Cutting out a section of a brown paper sack, she'd made a book cover for it, and dreaded the idea of any of the students at Hubert H. Humphrey middle school discovering what it was.

Right after school, she stopped to see Ms. Greer. "Good news and bad news," she said. "The good news is that I'll be able to help with the paper drive in two weeks, because I agreed to a different punishment."

"What's the bad news?" Ms. Greer looked at her full of concern.

"Oh, no, Ms. Greer, they didn't beat me."

"That's good. It breaks my heart when I think of all the abusive parents out there. It's really a barbarous practice, letting people be mothers just because they give birth to someone."

"The bad news is I have to memorize this book," Josalyn said, handing the book to her.

Ms. Greer opened the book, saw what it was, and broke into tears. "You poor woman," she said, pulling a tissue out of her well-worn tissue dispenser. "The nerve of your mother, forcing you to put all this pollution into your brain. You really have to memorize this garbage?"

"Yes. But my mother's not making me do it. It's that Mr. Minlow I told you about."

"Oh yes, the Christian. It figures. They feel they have the right to tell everyone how to behave."

"What can I do? He's a real hardhead."

"They talk about values, and manners. But whose values? And whose manners? Try asking him that. Young people should be free to choose what works best for them as individuals, and not have a bunch of ancient nonsense crammed into them."

Josalyn took the book back. "What if he refuses to be reasonable?"

"I'm afraid he probably will. They're like that. Then I suggest you be a good actor and suffer silently until this outrage is over."

5

"Hello, Miss Josalyn," Mr. Minlow said, as she came into her old bedroom.

"Hi," Josalyn said.

"Have you been studying the book?"

"Yes. I even showed it to Ms. Greer."

"Who is Ms. Greer?"

"She's the advisor to our Environment Club."

"Oh. I take it she's not enthused."

"You got it."

"I'll cry later."

"Uh, I have some questions about this thing."

"I thought you might."

"This is a really old book. It has nothing to with the reality I face every day."

"So you don't have anything to do with people?"

"I didn't say that. I just don't happen to have the values that are in this book."

"That's why I am having you memorize it. I feel you could use at least some of those values."

"But I don't want these values."

"You don't want to be nice to people? To make them feel good?"

"That's not my style. I prefer to open people's eyes to the stupid things they do."

"Why?"

"Because, because, well, I didn't mean it the way it sounded."

"You want to make a difference, don't you?"

"Yes. That's exactly it."

"And you think insulting people and making them feel bad is helping make a difference."

Josalyn seethed. This man was horrible. "I can't let you do it to me again."

"Do what?"

"Make me run out of the room screaming."

"That's good. I feel as though I've achieved something already."

"But don't be so smug, Mr. Minlow. I'll memorize your lousy rulebook, and serve out my sentence. But don't go thinking you're getting anywhere, because I'll just try to be a good actor."

"You mean actress."

"No. I mean actor. Ms. Greer explained that it's wrong for female actors to be called actresses just as it's wrong to call a female doctor doctress."

"Well, you and Ms. Greer are wrong about that."

"Oh, no, we're not."

"I was an actor before I was an evangelist."

"You expect me to believe that?"

"It's true. But what I'm trying to say is it probably is silly to call a female doctor a doctress, because gender is not usually a constant concern in medicine. But acting is different. Actors are often cast in parts not just for their talent, but also because they have to look something like the character they'll be playing. I mean, President Clinton is a man. It would be hard to accept a woman playing him in a movie. Even most extreme feminist leaders accept this. Actress is a nice convenient way to avoid saying male actor and female actor all the time. And I think it sounds nice. I don't know why you're so against girls and women."

"Me?" Josalyn asked. "Now I know you're crazy."

"Why are you so against indicating whether someone is female? Is it because you think boys are better, and it's a sign of weakness to be called a girl?"

Josalyn wanted to argue with him, but it was no use. He was better at it than her. "Why are you picking on me?"

"You're the one who keeps finding fault with me."

"You're wrong."

"There you go again."

"Why do you have to try to preach at me?"

"It's my job. Or it was."

Josalyn sighed. Winning an argument was impossible with this guy. First, he seemed so sure of himself, and had an answer for anything she might say.

Then, just when she was going to scream at him again, he said something that made her feel guilty.

"You have to understand," she said, "I like being in charge of my own life. I make my own choices."

"But you can't make any choices when you don't know where the buttons are."

"The what?"

"The buttons. Have you ever been in an elevator?"

"Of course."

"Well, what's the first thing you do when getting in one?"

"I stand still, looking ahead, not noticing anyone else."

"No, before that."

"I push the button for the floor I'm going to."

"How do you know which button to push?"

"They have numbers on them."

"But what if you were in an elevator, and there weren't any numbers on the buttons?"

"Well, I wouldn't know which one to push. I wouldn't be able to make a choice. I'd have to go complain somewhere."

"But you're wrong. You can make a choice. You can push any button you want."

"But I wouldn't know what floor I'd wind up"

"In other words, you couldn't make an informed choice. But let's say there's someone in the elevator with you. An adult, who was taught long ago which button is for what floor. Wouldn't you like to have him tell you what button goes to each floor? Just so you could make a better choice?"

"Yes."

"That's what I'm trying to do for you, Miss Josalyn. You're going to have to make many decisions in life, and it's easier if you know what the numbers are on the buttons. Otherwise, you won't go where you want to go. And I want you to go where you want to go."

"You do?"

"I want you to be happy."

"What's in it for you?"

He took a long look at the photo of his family. "I guess it's important for me to be a daddy to someone."

"Look, I'm sorry your family died in the car wreck. I'm sorry about what happened to you. But I don't need a daddy. I've done just fine without one until now. And even if I did want one, it wouldn't be you!" Josalyn ran out of the room, tears racing down her cheeks.

6

"I was going to have your mother talk with you, but she just called to say she wouldn't be home until late," Gram said, as she came into Josalyn's new room.

Josalyn barely looked up from where she was sitting on the side of her bed, her chin being held up by her hands.

"I suppose he told you," Josalyn said, waiting for Gram to let her have it.

"Yes, Mr. Minlow has sent you his apology, along with this book you left behind." Gram put the book of manners on the bed next to Josalyn.

"Apology?" Josalyn lifted her head.

"Yes. He feels he was too personal with you, and he's sorry about bringing up the business of being like a father to you."

"Is my punishment being extended?"

"No. Mr. Minlow insisted he was to blame for everything. Though from what I heard, you really should try to have more patience. That man's been through a lot. He can't help it if he's emotional sometimes."

"But he thinks he needs to preach at me."

"Maybe you should just let him. I mean, honey, Mr. Minlow really thinks a lot of you."

"You could have fooled me."

"You should hear what he says about you."

"What, that I'm a fool?"

"No. He thinks you're very smart."

"Really?"

"Really. And I know the real reason you don't like spending time with him."

"Yeah. Mr. Minlow is a crazy bigot."

"Oh, I'm sure you could put up with a guy who was totally wrong for a couple of weeks. But perhaps you're beginning to think he' might be right about some things. And that really scares you."

"What has that man ever been right about?"

"Well, he did say that you were smart." Gram smiled, and playfully touched the tip of Josalyn's nose. Josalyn smiled. Her grandmother was the only person she allowed to do that to her anymore. "You know, your mom and I just don't know where the time has gone. It doesn't seem as though it was that long ago that you were born. And now here you are, thirteen, and since your mom and I have both been hard at work, you've had to practically raise yourself."

"You and Mom have always been around enough."

"We've tried to be, but time has passed so quickly, and we've realized lately we've made a bad mistake."

"What mistake? Except for this awful punishment, I've got nothing to complain about. I love you guys."

"We love you too. But since your father left, there hasn't been much of a male presence around here."

"Gram, that man Mom married ran off when I was two. That shows you what men are made of. I'm glad Mom's never found the time to marry any of the guys she's dated."

"Josalyn, it won't be long before your opinion of men changes."

"My opinion will never change."

"I hope that doesn't happen, dear. We don't want you to turn out like those bitter women you're so found of."

"Oh, so now you're preaching at me, too."

"Don't raise your voice to me. I can still put you over my knees."

"Mom doesn't believe in spankings."

"She's real close to changing her mind about that, from the nasty little pill of a girl you've been lately."

Josalyn turned her back to her grandmother. "You don't know me at all."

"You don't know yourself, honey. You don't know what it means to care about people, and to do things for others."

"That's a lie. Everything I do is to make the world a better place."

"Sometimes the best thing a person can do is to make the world a happy place, and you certainly haven't been doing that lately. You have much to learn, honey."

"Like what?"

"Well, chew on this awhile. For all your complaining about Mr. Minlow, for all your gripes about what he thinks, and what he says to you, for all that, one thing is obvious. You like him."

"I do not."

"Do too."

"Do not.

"Do so."

"Gram, you're arguing like a kid."

"Am not." Josalyn couldn't keep a blank face anymore. "I'm glad to see you can still laugh," Gram said, laughing too. "When I say you like Mr. Minlow, I don't mean the way you like a cow licked boy at school. I mean the way you like a friend. Two people don't have to agree on everything to be friends, you know."

Gram left to check on Mr. Minlow, and Josalyn looked down at the book of manners. It was an absolutely ridiculous suggestion Gram had ever made, that Josalyn might possibly like such a horrible man. But as she picked up the book and started reading it, she knew it was true.

7

"Thank-you notes should be brief, but they should also be kind, cheerful and prompt," Josalyn recited. "Thank-you notes should be sent within a week of receiving a present."

"Very good," Mr. Minlow said. "Next section. That is, unless you haven't memorized it yet."

"Don't worry. It's in my head, and there it will stay. It's too weird to forget."

"Go ahead. Recite."

"Going out. Young ladies have to be proper hostesses at home, but when out in public it is the gentleman who takes over." Josalyn stopped reciting. "This has to be the most sickening part of this book," she exclaimed.

"Jump ahead to the rules, and recite those."

Josalyn wrinkled her nose and continued. "When finding seats at the movies, a boy always goes down the aisle in front of the girl to look for seats. He then allows the girl to sit first."

"Good, you seem to know this one as well as the others this week. Any questions? Why did you find this one so weird?"

"Boys and girls applaud differently," Josalyn said, reciting another part of that day's section. "A boy claps with the palms of his hand flat, but a girl forms a shallow cup of her left hand and spanks it with her right." Josalyn looked at Mr. Minlow with a smile that said 'gotcha.' "How can you possibly tell me that this is not totally sexist, as well as ridiculous?"

"Well, I guess it does sound silly, but think of it this way. The vast majority of girls and women have hands that are smaller than those of boys and men. Not all, but most. So if they applaud the same way men do, their applause will not be as loud. But if they cup one of their hands, they will achieve an equal loudness as that of the males."

"You think you're smart, don't you?" A few days before, Josalyn would have been yelling this at him. Now she was almost laughing.

"But this is what I've been trying to get across to you. I'm not against equality of the sexes. But women and men are different. Being different doesn't have to mean one is not as good as the other."

Josalyn decided to try to change the subject. "So, were you really an actor?"

"Yes."

"Did you make any money doing it?"

"Yes."

"Were you ever on TV, or in a movie?"

"Yes."

"Is yes the only answer I'm going to get? I mean, usually you talk my ears off Now that we're talking about something I'd like to hear about, all I get is yes."

"For most of my life I wanted to be an actor. In my early twenties, I worked in a lot of theatre. I was never famous. I usually played small parts in what they call road shows."

"Anything I've heard of?"

"Well, I was in the road show of Annie for a whole year. I even came through this city once with it." Josalyn tried not to roll her eyes, but she couldn't help it. "What's the matter? I take it you don't like Annie, either."

"Well, I don't remember it that well."

"Well, it's about this orphan girl, who brings happiness to a millionaire, who then adopts her."

"I think I saw a video of the movie when I was nine."

"The movie wasn't as good as the play."

"But the play still celebrates a stereotypical version of a little girl, doesn't it?"

"How do you mean?"

"I would have liked it much better if she had worn a pair of jeans instead of that red dress."

"Then she wouldn't have been Annie. What I always had a problem with was her curls. They really made her look like a baby," Mr. Minlow said.

"Well, those I understand. She sings that song about how she wishes she was somebody's baby, then, after she is adopted, she gets the curls, because she really is somebody's baby, instead of being an orphan. She has a daddy...." Josalyn stopped, but it was too late. Mr. Minlow had an extra sparkle in his eyes. He had led her right into a trap.

"You're right about the meaning of the curls. Now be honest with me, how many times have you watched Annie since you first saw it at nine?"

"Ten times," Josalyn mumbled, feeling very embarrassed. "It used to be one of my favorites."

"What's so wrong about that?"

"Everything. I was just too young to know better."

"I think I can guess why you like that movie."

"Oh, you can, huh?"

"I could see it on your face as you talked about her hair. You really identified with Annie. I bet you wished you could be like her, and find a Daddy to wear pretty dresses for."

"You're completely wrong. I hate dresses, and all they represent."

"What do they represent to you?"

"Look, I didn't know this was therapy. And if I did need counseling, I wouldn't be going to you."

"I just don't understand why you're so afraid of wearing a dress."

"To wear a dress is just the same thing as admitting that you're soft and weak."

"First, to be soft is not the same as being weak. It actually takes more strength to be gentle than to be a raging bull. And second, I wish you'd stop being so sexist."

"Me, stop being sexist? Now you've really lost all signs of intelligence."

"You're the one who keeps describing everything that's been traditionally associated with women as inferior to things traditionally male. As far as I'm concerned, it's the ultimate sign that a girl is happy being a girl when she wears a dress. A girl doesn't have to wear a dress to be a girl, but when she does it's like adding a big exclamation mark. She's saying I'm a girl, and not ashamed of it."

"I never said I was ashamed of being a girl."

"You know, your hair would look really good in curls. Do you ever wear your hair any way but pulled straight back?"

"Don't you dare talk about my hair."

"Yes, I can see it now. Perhaps not as tight as Annie's, but a good, loose set of curls. And bangs. And even a big hair ribbon or two, just so you'll be as pretty as possible."

"And you probably want me to put on a floral print dress, and white tights, just like you made your daughters do in that picture...." Josalyn gulped with guilt. "I'm sorry, but every time I start liking you, you do something to make me furious. When are you going to realize that this is 1992? The rules are different now. Bill Clinton is President."

"What I believe is just as true in 1992 as it was in the year one. And it will be just as true in 2092. What's right is rarely in fashion, but that doesn't change it from being right."

Josalyn glared at him. "You must love to see me run out of here angry. But I won't give you that pleasure, because my time is up for today." Josalyn walked out of the room before changing to a tearful run up the stairs.

8

"Josalyn, we can't talk long," Ms. Greer said the next morning. "Classes start in a couple of minutes."

"He's making me crazy, Ms. Greer."

"Who's that?"

"You know, the physically challenged man who's staying with us."

"Oh, yes. The Christian. What garbage is he trying to feed you now?"

"That I want to wear dresses and curl my hair."

"It figures. That's all any man seems to think women want to do. Did you explain that women are no longer the victims of men's sense of beauty, and are free to look as they please?"

"Do you really think all women are victims, Ms. Greer?"

Ms. Greer looked shocked that Josalyn would even ask the question. "Why certainly. Until we feminists started demanding equality, it was a man's world, and women were nothing but pretty little doormats."

"You mean, until the nineteen sixties, women amounted to nothing?"

"What's going on? Has that man been brainwashing you?"

The bell rang before Josalyn could answer. And as she ran to her homeroom, she wasn't sure anymore just who it was brainwashing her.

9

"I should have thought of this sooner," Josalyn thought, as she spent part of lunch period in the library. She had found a couple of books on etiquette, and they were both recently published. She leafed through the first book until she found the section she was looking for: *Ms., no matter how ugly its origin, is now the standard form for addressing a woman in a business setting. It has the advantage of not identifying a woman by her marital status, unlike the previous Miss\Mrs. system.* She knew it, Josalyn thought. She really had him now. Then she checked the other book: *It looks like we're stuck with Ms. It once was that a professional lady was called Mistress both before and after marriage. But then came a brief period where Mistress, in its shorter form Miss, was thought to define a single lady from a married one. So then came Ms.... Miss is* *short for Mistress, Mrs. is an abbreviation of Missus, however, Ms. is short for nothing. But we're stuck with Ms., which sounds like a bee's buzz when pronounced properly. So I suggest that people go on doing what they already are, writing it as Ms., but pronouncing it like Miss.* Josalyn snapped the book shut. Maybe this wasn't such a good idea after all.

10

"You seem extra distracted today," Mr. Minlow said.

"I'm okay," Josalyn said, as she sat in a chair at his bedside and continued to recite from the book of manners. "When you start to eat what you can't swallow, know how to take food out of your mouth. Remove fruit pits or chicken bones with your fingers. But non chewable meat must be removed with a fork, and placed on the side of your plate." Josalyn stopped reciting. "You know, this has to be the most sickening part of this whole book."

"Now what do you feel is sexist about dinner manners?"

"I didn't say it was sexist. I just said it's sickening." She hadn't told him about the extra research she had done on manners, and wasn't about to. But she had looked up something else she decided to bring to his attention. "I was in the library today."

"Good for you."

"I looked up your name in a movie guide. It wasn't in there."

"I only appeared in one film. It's not as if I was a big star or something."

"What was the name of the movie?"

"Promise you won't fall on the floor laughing?"

"Yes."

"I was in something called The Dragon that Ate Newark."

"I've never heard of it."

"Nobody else has, either."

"And it was about a dragon that ate Newark, New Jersey?"

"That's right. The movie was supposed to be bad intentionally, and it was. I was especially rotten. I was an ice cream man who served as an appetizer. Oh, so you find that funny?"

"I'm sorry," Josalyn said, laughing.

"You're probably thinking that devouring someone like me gave that dragon an awful case of heartburn."

"You said it, not me."

"I was paid two thousand dollars for being in that movie. The two thousand dollars is gone, but I got something else out of that film I can never lose."

"You mean being able to say you were in a movie?"

"No, I mean the humiliation. Sometimes I'll meet somebody who saw the thing late at night on television, and all I can do is apologize." Mr. Minlow winked at Josalyn, laughing, and Josalyn laughed some more, too.

"Why did you quit being an actor?"

"The Lord had a better job for me." Josalyn couldn't help making a face. "I take it you don't like mentioning God."

"I'm sorry; religion just doesn't do much for me."

"You could have fooled me."

"What do you mean?"

"Miss Josalyn, you're one of the most religious young ladies I've ever met."

"And you're one of the craziest men I've met. I'm not at all religious. I just don't see how people can believe in something they can't see, or touch."

"But you don't understand the meaning of the word religion," Mr. Minlow said. Josalyn sighed softly. "Religion literally means that which binds together. You can say it's what holds a person together. For most people, what binds their view of things together is God. But it doesn't have to be God. For some, I'm sad to say, their belief that there is no God is what holds them together."

"What's wrong with people believing there's no God?"

"Nothing, if there is no God. But wouldn't you agree that it would be terrible to not believe in God, when in fact there is a God?"

He was doing it to her again. He was so annoying. "Yes, I guess that would be bad, if God really does exist. But we have no way of knowing."

"Yes, we do."

"What, have you met God?"

"Yes. I have a personal relationship with him."

"Well, that's very good for you." Josalyn stood. "Are we finished for today?"

"Yes."

"See you tomorrow," Josalyn said, as she rushed out. Every time she started to like him, he seemed to become crazier.

11

"Try out some of the good manners you've been studying," Mr. Minlow had ordered. But as Josalyn walked down the school hallway, she didn't see how she could. Maybe people had manners when Mr. Minlow was in junior high. Maybe they all dressed perfectly, had lovely smiles, and were perfectly courteous. But as she watched her classmates shoving and pushing each other, and insulting each other with rotten names, she knew that manners were meaningless to them. But she didn't believe in lying, and she had to have something to report back to Mr. Minlow. Then she saw Claire, and she suddenly knew how to complete her assignment.

"Hi, Claire," she said, sliding up next to Claire.

"Hello," Claire said, not sounding very happy.

"Are you going to tell me I'm a loser because I wore a dress today?"

"I never said you were a loser, I just said...." Josalyn managed to stop herself in time. "What I wanted to say is I apologize, for how I treated you the other day."

Claire looked at Josalyn and her face brightened. "Really?"

Josalyn didn't understand why Claire's mood had changed so quickly. All she had said was that she apologized. But Claire looked as if she had just been given every dress in her size that the mall had. And Josalyn felt better too. “Really,” Josalyn said. “I’ve been thinking, maybe sometime we can get together and try on dresses, or something.”

Claire’s smile turned to a mock look of horror. “Who are you?”

“What?”

“You can’t be Josalyn Braden. You must a spy, cleverly made up to look like Josalyn.” Claire chuckled.

“No, I’m really Josalyn,” she insisted with a smile. And Claire suddenly seemed more a friend than ever before.

12

Josalyn was running late. She had stopped by Ms. Greer’s room to say she still planned to be involved with the paper drive, before racing down the hall so she could get home on time. Before she could go through the school door, however, a guy shoved his way in front of her. The boy was Eric Avery, the best all-round athlete in school. How Josalyn hated athletes. She disliked boys and men in general, but none more than sports jocks. They thought they were so hot. "Hey, you!" She yelled at Eric Avery.

"What do you want?" Eric said, turning to face her.

"I would like it if you showed a few manners."

"Manners?"

"Yes. A gentleman never shoves a lady out of the way in order to barge through a door ahead of her."

"Well, excuse me, Ms. Politeness."

"That's Miss Politeness to you, sir." Josalyn marched off, leaving Eric scratching his head.

13

"I even said we might get together to try on dresses," Josalyn said.

"You did?" Mr. Minlow asked, sounding shocked.

"But only because the book said it's good to express an interest in what others like. I still think the wearing of dresses is absolutely barbaric."

"Well, it's good that you've learned that little book of manners so well and so quickly," Mr. Minlow said.

Josalyn decided not to tell him about her encounter with Eric Avery. She hadn't planned to correct him on his manners, it had just happened. And she knew if she told Mr. Minlow about it, he would start thinking he was winning her over to his outdated beliefs, and that was the last thing she wanted. "So, are we done with this thing now?"

"Yes, I think you've learned what written in that book. If you use it is up to you."

"What are we going to do now?" Josalyn asked, though she wasn't sure she wanted to know.

"How about just talking?"

"About what?"

"I don't know. Why don't you decide?"

"I want to hear more about your acting."

"What about it?"

"Well, I know you left it behind. Haven't you ever missed being an actor?"

"Well, I never really stopped."

"Are you admitting you're a fake?"

"Oh, no," Mr. Minlow said, laughing. "I've always tried to be a real evangelist. I don't know if I've always been that good of one, but I've always tried to be real. And I've always used my skills as an actor in my evangelism."

"How?"

"Well, one thing I liked to do is tell stories. Would you like to hear one?"

"I'm a little old for storytelling."

"Nonsense."

"Excuse me?"

"Nobody's too old to listen to a good story."

"Well, go ahead. And I'll let you know whether or not it's good."

"I'm sure you will." Mr. Minlow closed his eyes for a second, and then he began to tell his story, with a voice that suddenly seemed stronger.

"Joe Alberti read over the letter he'd just composed, making certain it was perfect:

"Dear Elaine,

How are you, my wonderful girlfriend? I've missed you terribly since you left me. I can't seem to forget the way your platinum colored hair shines in the August sun, the way your eyes sparkle as they meet with mine. I still love you. As I write this I can hear the music of our song, "The Best of Times." This song never fails to make a tear or two come to my eyes. I am also burning a bowl of musk scented incense, the kind that you always liked to burn. It makes it almost seem as if you are here with me. Please come back to me. I need you so very much. As I write this I have my Bible in my hand. I know it is the Lord's Will that you come back to me. You're my lady, and I love you. I LOVE YOU.

Your guy forever, Joe Alberti."

Mr. Minlow paused for effect, and then continued.

"Joe placed the letter in an addressed, stamped envelope, sealed it, and dropped it in a mailbox as he went to work. He didn't much like his job, but being a graveyard janitor was the best he could do, since he didn't want to make any long term commitments until he found out how he stood with Elaine. They had met during their senior year of high school, and ever since then he'd known that she was the only one for him."

"This had better get good soon," Josalyn said.

"Don't interrupt," Mr. Minlow said. "It wrecks the mood." Mr. Minlow closed and opened his eyes again before continuing.

"Joe checked his mailbox every day for several weeks after mailing his letter to Elaine, but no response came. Then, just as he was starting to worry, a small white envelope arrived. Examining the return address, he saw that the letter was from Elaine. Hurrying back into his apartment, he started playing "The Best Of Times," lit up the musk scented incense, and sat at his kitchen table to read the special letter:

Dear Joe,

I really don't know what you expect me to say. It's been ages since we broke up. I've been married for some time now. I have a family.

But you? You've totally shut yourself off from the world. You work as a garbage man (or is it a janitor?), when you have all the talent to be a fine teacher. Remember how much you used to want to be one? And once a year, on the anniversary of our senior prom, I receive another pathetic little note from you, begging me to come back. Joe, we broke up fifteen years ago.

Enough is enough. You can still have a rewarding life, if you want to.

Elaine.

Joe's only reaction was to read the letter once again. Then, rising from his chair, he walked over to a nearby storage closet. Opening the closet door, he reached in and pulled out a shoe box. He pulled the lid off and smiled at the fourteen previous letters he had received from his girl. Grabbing the latest letter off the dining table, he read it once more. Same old Elaine, he thought, as he carefully slid the letter back into its shell and dropped it with the others in the shoe box. He then gathered together his recording of "The Best of Times," and whatever remained of the musk incense, and put everything away in the closet. He wouldn't need them again until next year."

"That's it?"

"Yeah. What'd you think?"

"I don't know. I guess it's interesting, but what does it mean?"

"It means don't wreck your present and future by agonizing over things that didn't work out in the past."

"But why did you tell this story to me?"

"It's just something designed to provoke thought. You don't have to read anything personal into it."

"You think I should forget about my father, and how he left, don't you?"

"I don't think you should forget your father."

"Well, good, because the only thing I really know about my father is that he left, and I'll never forget that."

"I know, honey."

"Don't call me honey."

"Okay, Miss Josalyn. But I don't know why we can't be friends."

"Because we don't agree on anything."

"Sometimes the best of friends actually have little they completely agree on."

"Look, you know how I feel about things. Why do you want to be friends with someone who thinks you're wrong about everything?"

"That's what we have in common. We each think the other is wrong."

Josalyn smiled. "Okay. If you want to think of me as your friend, I'll try to think of you as one, too. But just don't spread it around. I've got my reputation to think about."

14

April, 1992

"Miss Josalyn, what's wrong?" Mr. Minlow asked, as a sad faced Josalyn slumped into the chair at the side of his bed.

"Today was the last day of the paper drive," Josalyn said, unable to keep her voice from quivering.

"I thought you were doing great."

"I was, at least I thought. I won. I arranged for twice as much paper donations as anyone else."

"Then what's wrong?"

"Ms. Greer put me down. She insulted me right in front of everyone."

"What did she say?"

"She, she...."

"Breathe deep, and exhale slowly." Josalyn did so. "Now, what happened?"

"I thought getting people to donate their old newspapers was what the paper drive was all about. But we all had this speech we were supposed to deliver when people opened their doors. The speech was full of stuff about how wasteful everyone lives, and how we need to stop being such pigs. A few weeks ago I wouldn't have thought anything of saying this to people. But now, well, it just seemed so rude. Anyway, Ms. Greer asked me about people's reaction to the speech, and when I told her I didn't use it, she said I had totally failed."

"Oh, dear. I see that I'm responsible for all this. I had to go and teach you some manners. I tell you what, why don't you lay one right on my chin."

"What?"

"You heard me. Slug me. Get revenge for my having ruined your career."

Josalyn couldn't help smiling. "Violence is never an answer," she said, stifling a giggle.

"Ah, but just the thought of it makes you smile."

"I'm not smiling at the thought of hitting you. It's just that, you're so, so ridiculous."

"You're not the first to tell me that about myself." Mr. Minlow rolled his eyes teasingly, and Josalyn couldn't hold back her giggles. "What's so funny? I thought just a moment ago you were the saddest girl in the world."

"I just can't believe you sometimes."

Josalyn couldn't believe herself sometimes, either. She really had come into the room all depressed. But Mr. Minlow, without really trying, had made her feel better. This was crazy, Josalyn thought. But as she stood there giggling, she realized that, however different he was from her, she loved Mr. Minlow with all her soul.

15

"We're sorry to see you go," Ms. Greer had said. But Josalyn knew she didn't mean it. She never thought she would ever quit the environment club, and as she walked down the hall from Ms. Greer's room, she still couldn't believe she had. But she didn't have much choice. In the week since the paper drive ended, she hadn't felt as though she belonged there anymore. She thought the whole point of the paper drive was to collect newspapers for recycling, thereby helping the environment. But she had collected more newspapers than anyone else, only to be called a loser. It didn't seem that long ago that she knew everything. Now she didn't feel as if she understood anything.

"Allow me, ma'am," Eric Avery said, as he appeared out of nowhere to open the school door for Josalyn.

"Look, I've been through enough already without you making fun of me," Josalyn said. "I'm sorry I got on you about manners and all."

"I'm not making fun of you, Josalyn," Eric said, sounding hurt.

"Why aren't you out doing push-ups with the other jocks?"

"I got hurt," he said, holding up a bandaged hand.

"Is it bad?"

"Nah. I just have to be careful for a week or so."

"Well, I have to be getting home," Josalyn said, taking a step forward.

Eric closed his eyes, and spoke really fast. "Josalyn, I was wondering if I could buy you a pop over at Burger Barons."

A goofy feeling came over Josalyn as she realized what was going on. Eric liked her! She didn't know what to say, and all she felt like doing was running. So that's what she did, without looking back, until she was two whole blocks away. By the time she arrived home, not only did she feel as if she didn't know anything anymore, she also felt like a total fool.

16

"Miss Josalyn, what happened?" Mr. Minlow said, as Josalyn dragged herself into his room. "You look like you just ran a marathon."

"I did." Josalyn, controlling the tears that wished to explode from her eyes, told Mr. Minlow everything.

"So a boy wanted to buy you a pop, and it really scared you," Mr. Minlow said.

"Yeah."

"And it scared you because you liked it."

"Yeah. Up to now, whenever a boy said he liked me, I just told him to go away."

"Miss Josalyn, you're thirteen. You're supposed to like boys just a little more than you did when you were younger."

"I guess you're right."

"But just a little bit. You don't have to rush it."

"I don't?"

"Of course not. You're still a little girl."

Though she was glad he had said it, Josalyn couldn't let him know it. "I'm not a little girl, and don't you go calling me one," she said. But it was hard to keep from smiling.

"Just the same, I'm sure your mother, if asked, would tell you that you're still too young to go out on nighttime dates, or go steady. But having a pop after school is fine. Be sure to tell him that your mom is really old fashioned, and won't let you start having formal dates just yet."

"Okay," Josalyn said. She thought about what some of the kids in her class were already doing, and how funny it was that Mr. Minlow didn't have any idea what kids did now. But she also felt relieved that she had been told she couldn't do those things. It dawned on her that maybe the kids in her class who were grossly involved with the opposite sex didn't have a mother or father telling them not to be. Then her relief turned to gloom, as she remembered how she had acted. "He probably doesn't like me anymore. I mean, the way I ran away, he must think I'm emotionally disturbed."

"Take my word for it; he doesn't think you're crazy."

"He doesn't?"

"He just thinks you're a girl."

"Are you ever going to stop being such a sexist?" she asked, with a big smile she could no longer keep hidden.

"I'll never stop loving the wonderful way God made men and women different." He smiled, and Josalyn saw he was looking at the picture of his wife and daughters. "I'll never forget the first time I saw my wife, Cheryl. I had just finished telling a story in front of a church of eight-hundred people. The service was over, and as the choir and the congregation sang the last hymn, the pastor and I were to walk down the center aisle out to the lobby, where we would stand and greet people as they left the church. Only I didn't even make it down the platform steps."

"What happened?"

"I tripped, and landed on my back."

"Were you hurt?"

"Only my pride was injured. People in the congregation rushed around me, but I only could see one of them."

"Cheryl?"

"Yes. There she was, so beautiful, looking at me with much concern. It turned out she was the daughter of the pastor. For me, it was a crush at first sight. But she didn't like me at first. Only when I fell."

"What do you mean?"

"She had enjoyed my story, but she'd heard plenty of good stories. She didn't think I was much different from all the other evangelists she had seen. But when I took that tumble, she said she knew I was all boy."

"You must really miss your family," Josalyn said softly, unable to keep herself from asking.

Mr. Minlow was silent for a moment. "I sure do."

“I’m sorry; I shouldn’t have brought it up.”

“Don’t worry; you haven’t caused me any pain. Memories of my family only bring me happiness. Mandy, my oldest girl, would be ten now. She was a big-time reader. She loved to climb in my lap and tell me all about the latest book she’d read. And Janie, who would be nine, was my little rascal. She liked to sneak up behind me and scare me. And how she loved horses. I was always on the lookout for anything horse related I could bring home to her. I remember once I found this little model of a Pinto, her favorite type of horse. And now, whenever I find it hard to smile, I remember the look on Janie’s little face when I gave her that tiny doll....”

“How can you smile at all?” Josalyn asked. “I couldn’t, if I were you.”

“The reason I can smile, Miss Josalyn, is that I try not to think about how much I miss them. Instead, I smile because I know they’re with the Lord.”

“But God took them away from you.”

"No. God gave them to me. A drunk driver took them away."

"Couldn't God have stopped the drunk driver?"

"He could have. But you have to understand; in this world God has given us all free will."

"Free will?"

"Yes. We are free to not follow God's will, to follow instead our own whims and aims."

"And you don't think it's good to go your own way in life?"

"No. It always leads to unhappiness and evildoing."

"Evildoing? Give me a break. You sound like some guy in an old horror movie."

"It's strange how the word evil sounds funny to people. But what would you call what happened to my family and me, if not evil?"

"I guess you're right."

"The Lord's Will for that man wasn't for him to drink half a bottle of scotch and get behind the wheel of his car. Especially since his license had already been taken away for doing it in the past."

"I can understand you hating him, but alcoholism is a disease."

"I don't hate him. I hate evil. Evil was at work on his soul, and that made him take his very first drink, though he had to know it might lead him down the road to alcoholism."

"Are you talking about the devil?"

"Who else? That's whom I reserve my hatred for."

"Why is it every discussion we have turns into a church service?"

"I wouldn't call it a church service. I mean, we never sing. I'd say it was more like Sunday school."

"I'm not going to let you joke your way out of this. You're trying to change me into your idealized image of a sweet little Christian girl, and I just can't be that."

"Miss Josalyn, I just want you to be as happy as possible. What you believe is up to you. I just think it's important that you believe in something, whatever it may be."

Mr. Minlow paused. “You didn’t roll your eyes.”

“I guess you’ve got a point,” Josalyn said. She still hadn’t won an argument with him.

17

“I’ll have a large lemon-lime, please,” Josalyn said.

“And I’ll have an extra large Sportaide,” Eric said to the counter girl at Burger Barons.

“I’m sorry, we don’t have Sportaide,” the counter girl said.

“Oh, yeah. I forgot,” Eric said, looking embarrassed. “I’ll take lemon-lime, too. Just like the lady.”

Josalyn smiled nervously. Mr. Minlow had been right. Eric had accepted her apology for running off, and had invited her out for a pop again. And as they had walked the three blocks to Burger Barons, Eric had gone to extremes with the manners stuff. He had opened doors for her, and had insisted on walking on the street side of the sidewalk. And now he was paying for both their drinks. "I wonder why they have to know what kind of pop we want," she said, as they took their empty cups to the pop dispenser. "I mean, we have to fill them ourselves anyway."

"My father told me that it's because they need to keep track of how much they sell of each kind, ma'am."

A nervous silence lingered as they each filled their cups with lemon-lime and sat in a booth. "Uh, Eric," Josalyn finally said.

"Yes, ma'am?"

"Why do you keep calling me ma'am?"

"It said in the etiquette book I read to call all ladies ma'am."

"You read an etiquette book?"

"Well, what you said the other day was true. I didn't know any manners. When I hurt my hand, I had some spare time, so I read the book my parents had. Don't you like me calling you ma'am?"

"Well, to be honest, I think I'm not old enough yet. I mean, I'm still a little.... I'm still just a kid. Did you really study manners just to impress me?"

"No, you impressed me. Can I tell you a secret? You're the first girl I've ever done anything like this with."

"You're kidding. I mean, every girl in school thinks you're cute."

"They do? Well, I think I like old-fashioned girls like you."

Josalyn was amazed. "You think I'm old-fashioned? Me?"

"Well, yeah. You know all about manners, and you ran off when I first asked you out."

"What's old-fashioned about running away scared?"

"My mom is really old-fashioned, and she did the same thing when a guy asked her out for the first time. She likes to joke about it."

Josalyn smiled, and a strange feeling came over her as she realized she liked

Eric not just for his good looks. She liked him because, in some ways, he reminded her of Mr. Minlow.

18

"I'm glad you had a good time," Mr. Minlow said. His voice was whispery; much as it had been on the day he had arrived.

"Are you sure you're okay?" Josalyn asked.

"Oh, yes. It's just that once in a while, when I get tired, it's hard for me to make my lungs work."

"Do you want Gram to put on your respirator for you?"

"No, I hate that thing."

Josalyn looked down at Mr. Minlow, and couldn't stop worrying about him. She had come straight into his room after Eric had walked her home.

She had to tell him about it even before she told Gram. But he looked as bad as he sounded. His face was ashen, and covered with perspiration. She was so excited she had just bounded into the room and told him how great it had been. Then she had taken a good look at him, and forgot all about Eric. But she kept a smile on her face, and tried to pretend with him that nothing was wrong. "I was kind of hoping to hear another story from you today."

"I thought you hated the last one I told you."

"They sort of grow on you."

"Josalyn, please leave now," Gram sternly said, as she rushed into the room, followed by two paramedics.

Horrified, Josalyn didn't want to move. But then Mr. Minlow's lungs began to heave, and he gasped for air. Josalyn collapsed in a corner as the paramedics stuck Mr. Minlow's respirator on, before lifting him onto the gurney they had brought. By now Mr. Minlow had lost consciousness, and Josalyn couldn't even say goodbye as the paramedics loaded him into the ambulance and drove off, sirens blaring.

"Is he going to be okay?" Josalyn asked Gram.

"I wish I could tell you that, dear, but I don't think so. The doctors have thought all along that he was just one bout of pneumonia away from leaving us."

"No, he can't die!" Josalyn shouted, as she took off up the stairs. Collapsing face down on her bed, she sobbed and cried. Mr. Minlow was going to die, and she hadn't told him how she really felt. She loved him, and needed him to be.... her Daddy. Having finally admitted to herself how she really felt about him, Josalyn sobbed again. Then, an inspiration came to her. Maybe it wasn't too late. Maybe if she went to him, and showed him how much she wanted to be his child, just maybe that would give him the strength he needed to hang on. But she couldn't go straight to the hospital.

"Josalyn," Gram said, as Josalyn came down the stairs. "I'm going to the hospital, and you can come with me if you want."

"I'll be there in a little while," Josalyn said, opening the front door. "I have to go to Claire's down the street first. It's really important." And before Gram could try to stop her, Josalyn was racing down the sidewalk.

19

"You really look nice this way, Josalyn," Claire said, buttoning up the back of the dress Josalyn had just slipped into.

"I don't know about that," Josalyn softly mumbled.

"It's just a good thing we wear the same dress size."

"I'm glad that at least I can squeeze into these black flats of yours," Josalyn said, sitting on the side of her bed and smoothing out her new white tights before slipping on the shoes. She stood and looked at herself again in Claire's wall mirror. "I really appreciate all your help, Claire."

"It's my pleasure. I never thought I'd ever see you done up like this."

"I never thought so, either. I used to think dresses and hair ribbons were ridiculous and sexist." Josalyn reached up and touched the bright bows Claire had put in her hair. And she smiled.

"I can't believe you let me cut and curl your hair like that. It's going to be impossible to put it back, you know."

"Then I won't put it back."

"You must really think a lot of that Mr. Minlow, to get dressed a way you don't like."

"Yeah," Josalyn said quietly. And she said little more as Claire's mother drove her to the hospital.

20

"Josalyn...." Her mother, stunned at her appearance, slid back into her chair near the door. But all Josalyn was looking at was Mr. Minlow. His eyes were closed, and he was still breathing with difficulty as the doctor and nurses worked on him.

"That's it, there's nothing more we can do," the doctor said.

"What do you mean there's nothing more you can do?" Josalyn asked.

"The pneumonia's just too much for what lungs he has, honey," Gram said, the lines on her face deep with sadness.

"Why have you taken off his respirator?"

"His lungs are far gone for it to help, young lady," the doctor said.

"Josalyn, let's go out to the waiting room, we can't do any good in here," Mom said, leaving.

"No, he can't die," Josalyn said to Gram. "I've got to stay here and have him see me."

"He may not regain consciousness," the doctor said.

"He's got to wake up; he's got to know...." Josalyn was too choked with tears to continue.

"Then you'd better stay right here," Gram said, giving Josalyn a hug. Gram pulled a chair to the side of the bed, and motioned for Josalyn to sit in it.

"This way, if he opens his eyes, he'll see you first."

Josalyn sat in the chair. The doctor and Gram sat in the back of the room. She wished the doctor would leave. Josalyn knew the only reason she was staying was that she thought Mr. Minlow didn't have long. Otherwise, the doctor would be rushing off where she could be more useful. Josalyn found it difficult to be brave as she sat staring at Mr. Minlow's ashen face, and listened to the faint but awful sounds of him struggling to breathe. Then, just as she had hoped, just as she had prayed, his breathing became less labored, and his head moved slightly. Gram and the doctor stood up, but did not come closer, as Mr. Minlow opened his eyes. Josalyn stood up. "Mr. Minlow?" she asked.

"That's who I am," he said in barely a whisper. His eyes examined her, and the more he looked at her, the bigger his smile got. Mr. Minlow always had a big smile, but not like now. She'd never seen a smile so big, and his whole face suddenly was glowing. "But who is this pretty little girl I'm looking at?"

"It's me, Josalyn."

"Well, what's the reason for this?"

Josalyn knew that Gram and the doctor were listening, but she didn't care. "You're the reason. I wanted to dress the way I thought you'd like to see me. You see, I even have on white tights," she said, pulling up her hem a bit.

"You cut your hair into bangs."

"My friend Claire did it."

"Those are the prettiest curls I've ever seen. But you're not going to be able to pull your hair back as easily."

"I don't want to wear it like that any more. I'm not the same as I was when you first met me. Until you came along, I didn't really know who I was. Now I do. I'm your kid.... your little girl. So you had better not be going anywhere. I mean, you wouldn't want to leave a poor helpless little girl without a daddy, would you?"

"You've never been helpless. But I'm afraid it's not my choice whether I stay."

"But you can't leave. I need you. I love you, Daddy." Josalyn kissed him on his cheek.

"I love you too, my daughter. Always remember that wherever you go, whatever you do, you will never be alone. My love will always be there with you. And if you're faithful, and trust in the Lord, someday we'll see each other again."

"But Daddy, I need you now," Josalyn said, tears running down her cheeks.

"I'll never stop loving you, Miss Josalyn," Mr. Minlow said, his voice barely audible.

"No, Daddy," Josalyn said, leaning in really close to hear what he might say next.

But he said nothing. She heard a buzzing sound, but she ignored it as her teary eyes stared into his, and he stared intently back, his eyes full of happiness. Then Josalyn felt something touch her face. His hand. He ran his fingers gently along her cheek, then, just as suddenly, his arm went limp again, and Josalyn became aware of the doctor leaning over from the other side of the bed, checking Mr. Minlow's pulse with her stethoscope. The buzzing sound she heard was coming from the heart monitor. The wavy line that had been there was now flat.

"He's dead," the doctor said.

"No!" Josalyn cried. She buried her head in his chest, sobbing uncontrollably.

21

"How are you doing, honey?" Gram asked, coming into Josalyn's room.

"Fine, for a crazy, I mean emotionally ill person." Josalyn was sitting on the side of her bed, still in the black dress she'd worn to Mr. Minlow's funeral that afternoon.

"You're not crazy," Gram said, sitting next to her.

"Then why doesn't anyone believe me? He reached up and caressed my face with his hand before he died."

"I was there, honey, and I didn't see it."

"I know. He was paralyzed, and besides, the machines all said he was already dead when it happened. But I saw it. I felt it." Josalyn looked up, and noticed the box Gram had brought in with her.

"What's that?"

"They are some of Mr. Minlow's things. Last week, before anyone knew he was so ill, he told me that you were to have these. And there's a tape he made, too."

"A tape? What did he say?"

"I don't know. He made me leave the room, and I haven't listened to it." Leaving the box on the bed, Gram stood. "We've about cleared out your old room. Whenever you want, you can start moving back in."

Gram left, and Josalyn started crying again. That room now belonged to Mr. Minlow. She didn't think she could handle being in there ever again. She saw the tape on top of the things in the box, and pulled it out. She stared at Gram's writing on the case. For Josalyn, it said. She stuck the tape carefully into her music machine, and started it.

"Hello, Miss Josalyn," Mr. Minlow said. "Since you're hearing this, I must either be dead, or you've been a terrible little brat and stolen this tape from your grandmother." Josalyn couldn't help smiling through her tears. "But I doubt it's the latter, because you're such a good kid. I guess you're having a pretty hard time of it now. But I want you to know, that even if you never did get around to saying it, I know that you loved me and that you even think of me as a father, though you claimed you never would. You see, little girls can't hide how they feel about their fathers. Or men they want to be their fathers." He'd already known how she felt, even before she told him, or showed him. But she was still glad she had. "I guess you've been doing a little crying." A little? "That's okay. It's okay to be sad right now. I know I'm going to really miss our visits; I can't blame you if you miss me too. But you mustn't allow what happened to me to keep you from living your life to the fullest. I know you didn't like talking about religion, so you can shut off this tape at this point if you want."

No chance of that, Josalyn thought.

"When I die, I know I'll go to a wonderful place. What paralyzed me in the world, what made me sad, will only be a memory. The only thing can possibly make me sad is if the daughter I left behind fails to find the happiness that God has in mind for her. The Lord has many wonderful things in store for you, Miss Josalyn. I can't tell you exactly what they all are, because they are something each person has to discover for themselves. But based on what I know about you, I can give you some hints. You're the sort of girl who will find happiness in making others happy. Make others happy, and I know you'll discover that the biggest smile is your own."

Mom stuck her head in the door, and Josalyn stopped the tape. "I was going to tell you that it's time for dinner, but I can see you're busy."

"I'll be down in a few minutes, Mom. And Mom?"

"Yes, honey?"

"I sure do love you."

Mom's face exploded into a smile. "I love you, too," she said, sounding as if she was going to cry.

After she left, Josalyn restarted the tape. "I wish I could be around to see the wonderful woman you're going to become. But there's something special about love. We never lose love once we create it. Either we forget it exists, or it was never real to begin with. Please know that no matter what, my love for you will always exist. Wherever you go, or what you do, my love will be with you. You cannot, however you try, lose my love. You will always be my little girl." Mr. Minlow's voice trailed off, and Josalyn could hear that he was crying. She heard Gram's voice in the background, followed by the sound of the tape recorder being turned off.

When the recorder started again, his voice was steady again. "But while I can't be there for you except through my love, you're not fatherless. It's my love, my love for you. Please always remember, that love will never go away." There was a pause, then he called out "Mrs. Braden, I'm finished." This was followed by the sound of Gram walking back into the room, before the recorder was shut off for the final time.

Josalyn reached back into the box, and pulled out the picture of Daddy and his wife, Cheryl. And his other two daughters, Mandy and Janie. And she knew they were all together and happy now. She reached up and felt the part of her face her Daddy had touched. She was still learning what she believed, however, she had no doubt in the reality of love, and the powerful things it could do. Love, she now knew, was as real as Daddy's touch. After all, just because people can't see something, it doesn't mean it's not real.

Also by Jane Comer

Really, Truly, Katherine Beagan

It's 1987, and everyone has an opinion of fifteen-year-old Katherine Beagan. To her therapist she's emotionally disturbed, while her principal thinks she is a trouble-maker. To her classmates she's a runt, while her social worker thinks she's a punk. But when the Portland police call her an arson, her only escape is to pretend to be someone else, and that is when her real trouble begins....

Really, Truly, Katherine Beagan blends Anne of Green Gables with Ferris Bueller, TV comedies with real life struggles, and shows that happiness can arrive by following the most unexpected paths.

About the Author

Jane Comer, writer and actress, believes in the power of human communication. From Portland, Oregon, she makes connections in between dodging the rain.

www.ingramcontent.com/pod-product-compliance
Lightning Source LLC
LaVergne TN
LVHW010946110826
845149LV00015B/3235